HOUSE

$\sim\sim of \sim\sim$

DOLLS

ALSO BY FRANCESCA LIA BLOCK:

Weetzie Bat

Missing Angel Juan

Girl Goddess #9: Nine Stories

The Hanged Man

Dangerous Angels: The Weetzie Bat Books

I Was a Teenage Fairy

Violet and Claire

The Rose and the Beast

Echo

Guarding the Moon

Wasteland

Goat Girls: Two Weetzie Bat Books

Beautiful Boys: Two Weetzie Bat Books

Necklace of Kisses

Psyche in a Dress

Blood Roses

How to (Un)cage a Girl

The Waters & the Wild

Pretty Dead

FRANCESCA LIA BLOCK

HOUSE

of

DOLLS

ILLUSTRATED BY

BARBARA MᶜCLINTOCK

HARPER
An Imprint of HarperCollinsPublishers

Library of Congress Cataloging-in-Publication
Data Block, Francesca Lia. House of dolls /
Francesca Lia Block ; illustrated by Barbara
McClintock. — 1st ed.   p.   cm.
Summary: Madison Blackberry's dolls—
Wildflower, Rockstar, and Miss Selene—have
lives that she envies, with their beautiful
clothes and warm, cozy house, while she is
lonely most of the time.
ISBN 978-0-06-113094-6
[1. Dolls—Fiction. 2. Dollhouses—
Fiction. 3. Loneliness—Fiction.]
I. McClintock, Barbara, ill. II. Title.
PZ7.B61945Ho 2010   2009020694
[Fic]—dc22   CIP
                                            AC
Typography by Torborg Davern
❖
First Edition

10 11 12 13 14   SCP   10 9 8 7 6 5 4 3 2 1

For the Littles
—F.L.B.

To Jennie
—B.M.

part one

THE
DOLLS

Wildflower,
Rockstar,
and Miss Selene
lived in a house
from another time,
a white house with a
red roof and
red shutters and a
red front door.

In the garden was a real bonsai tree and a reflecting pool made from a pocket mirror tucked into a lawn of real moss. The floors were tiled with black-and-white parquet or softly carpeted, and the walls were covered with floral paper, foil mirrors, and paintings in gold doily frames. Above the dining room table was a silver chandelier fixed with birthday candles. Silk and lace curtains hung at every window.

The house belonged to Madison Blackberry, a tall-for-her-age, sour-faced girl who secretly wished, more than almost anything, that she could live in the dollhouse with the dolls. They seemed so warm and cozy, and

4

they nestled so closely together among the black-and-rose needlepoint pillows on the green velvet chaise longue in the parlor, as if they never wished to be apart.

This was very different from life in the cool, all-white-and-gray penthouse apartment where Madison Blackberry lived with her mother, father, and little brother, Dallas George.

Because the dolls made Madison Blackberry feel lonelier than she already was, she ignored them most of the time. The dolls didn't mind. They spent their days enjoying the company of one another as well as Wildflower's boyfriend, Guy, and Rockstar's boyfriend, B. Friend, and trying on the clothes that Madison Blackberry's grandmother sewed for them.

The dollhouse had belonged to Madison's grandmother when she was a girl. Her father had made it. She and her mother had played with it together. Wildflower had belonged to Madison's grandmother, too.

Wildflower was a celluloid doll with long black braids of real hair, pale skin, and big brown eyes with painted-on eyelashes. Guy was a dark-skinned plastic doll in army fatigues. It did not matter that they looked nothing alike. The first time Madison Blackberry lay them down next to each other in the

white lace canopy bed and their arms brushed, Wildflower and Guy knew they never wanted to be separated. Because Wildflower had lived so long and seen so much of the world, she would have been content just to sit beside Guy for the rest of her existence.

Rockstar had been given to Madison Blackberry one Hanukkah and she had been a huge disappointment. Madison Blackberry had wanted a more glamorous doll with a lipstick-red mouth, sunglasses, and high heels, but instead she was given the meek, mousy-haired girl with the plastic head, hands, and feet, and the bendable wire body swaddled in linen like a small mummy.

7

Madison Blackberry named her Rockstar, as a way to remind herself of her mother's injustice, and perhaps as a way to punish the doll for being so plain and much too intelligent for someone with a plastic head. Rockstar would have preferred the name Lillian or Rebecca or Emily Sarah, but as it was, she tried to enjoy the irony of Rockstar and sometimes had fun dressing the part anyway. She longed to pick up the books in the library and read them but was afraid to get caught by Madison Blackberry, who was already frustrated enough with her.

But Rockstar had no idea why Madison Blackberry felt that way.

B. Friend was a devastatingly handsome stuffed bear with button eyes, an embroidered nose, and jointed arms and legs. He was a studious fellow with round wire-rimmed glasses with lenses made of a clear dried nail polish. B. Friend wore a red crochet beret and a red flannel vest and britches. Madison Blackberry had originally named him Boyfriend, but because he was not really a boy, the dolls called him B. (as in bear) Friend for short.

Miss Selene was a delicately crafted fairy with golden curls, pointed ears, lavender eyes, greenish skin, and silver wings. She did not have a boyfriend, but she loved to dream up ideas

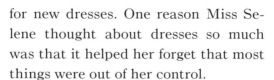

for new dresses. One reason Miss Selene thought about dresses so much was that it helped her forget that most things were out of her control.

Madison Blackberry's grandmother had crocheted the runner that went all the way up the polished wood staircase that led to the nursery with the empty cradle, and she had sewed all the silk and lace curtains at the windows. The dresses she made for the dolls were ornate concoctions,

interpretations of styles from every era. There were dresses that made the dolls feel like ice-cream sundaes, flowers, seashells, cocoons, butterflies, angels, goddesses, rock stars, heavenly stars, and moons. In their spellbinding dresses the dolls spent their evenings talking, singing, dancing, and baking tiny play-dough cakes with Guy and B. Friend.

The dolls also delighted in small things like putting the china teacups with blue roses away in the wooden sideboard, pouring water out of the real glass pitcher with gold filigree into the matching glasses, arranging papers and pencils in the rolltop desk,

11

sniffing the lingering fragrance in the real perfume bottles with dove-shaped stoppers on the glass-topped dressing table, folding their sweaters into the pink-rose paper-lined drawers, and hanging up their dresses on the miniature wooden hangers in the wooden wardrobe.

Sometimes Madison Blackberry's grandmother gave them real lemonade in the glass pitcher, and, instead of a play-dough cake, she gave them one of the real chocolates from her birthday or Valentine's Day box. The coating crumbled a little when they put the birthday candle in, and they could see the mystery of the secret filling—

cream or caramel or more chocolate inside. And for many weeks after, they could smell the chocolate on the brown crinkly wrapper.

Life was small but good.

But then, one day, as things always do—even for dolls—everything changed.

part two

MADISON
BLACKBERRY

Madison
Blackberry
was bored.
Her grandmother
said that no
one should ever
be bored,
life was too rich,
too full;
there was always
something more
to do.

But Madison Blackberry was bored in her fancy all-white-and-gray apartment that rose so high above the city that the world below looked less real than her dollhouse. She was bored with her fancy toys, bored without any friends to play with. For the dolls, Madison Blackberry's boredom was a terrible thing to behold.

And not only was Madison Blackberry bored, Madison Blackberry was jealous.

She was jealous of her little brother, Dallas George, who was the baby and got all the attention and was never punished for scaring her with his toy soldiers. She was jealous of her mother, who sailed out the door on puffy, sweet clouds of chiffon and perfume to fund-raisers and galas, and who never had time to play with or read to her. She was jealous of her father, who, it seemed, didn't have to do what any-one else in the world said. Who could travel all over the world and stay away as long as he chose and buy whatever he wanted.

Madison Blackberry was especially jealous of the dolls.

For many years Wildflower had been kept in a box in Madison Blackberry's mother's closet. Madison Blackberry was only allowed to touch her with one finger on special occasions because she was "valuable" and a "family heirloom." This had caused an early resentment toward Wildflower.

Even after Madison Blackberry's grandmother convinced her mother to let Wildflower come out and live in the dollhouse, Madison Blackberry still felt her fingers stiffen when she touched Wildflower. She knew that if anything ever happened to the doll she would have to witness her mother's anger, and, although it rarely presented

itself, it was not something anyone in the house wanted to behold.

Madison Blackberry resented Rockstar because she knew, with a young, female doll owner's intuition, that Rockstar was smarter than she was.

Madison Blackberry resented Miss Selene because of her golden curls, her pointed ears, her lavender eyes, and especially her delicately crafted silver wings.

The combination of boredom and jealousy is a dangerous thing. Especially when the person feeling these things is so many times larger than you are.

The result was this: Madison Blackberry sent Guy off to war.

23

Madison did not feel there was room in the house for Guy. And, after hearing her father listening to the news, she wanted some drama for her dolls.

The dolls did not know that "war" was really a dusty box in a closet of the apartment where the dollhouse lived. It didn't matter. As far as Guy and Wildflower were concerned, that *was* war.

War was life without each other.

Then B. Friend was pronounced MIA by Madison Blackberry. One of his jointed arms had been torn from his body by Madison Blackberry's little brother, Dallas George. Stuffing came out of his furry body as he lay in Dallas George's toy chest among the plastic machine guns and airplanes. His arm was chewed into an unrecognizable pulp by the dog. His glasses were stepped on and twisted beyond recognition. Not even the cleaning lady had discovered B. Friend. In spite of his broken state, he dreamed of Rockstar day and night in his world of shadows and dust balls.

After the disappearance of Guy, Wildflower was no longer interested in dresses, dancing, or baking play-dough cakes. She wanted, instead, to change the world.

This was not the first time Wildflower had become concerned with changing the world. She had felt the

same way, years before, during another war, when she belonged to
Grandmother.

But then, as now, she did not know
what to do.

After the disappearance of B. Friend,
Rockstar was no longer interested in
dresses, singing, dancing, or baking
play-dough cakes. She wanted
to change herself.

She had been rejected
by Madison Blackberry
because she was too intelligent, but Rockstar had
never even
taken the
time to

enjoy her own intellect! She got hold of all the miniature leather-bound books in the dollhouse bookcase and began to read them one by one.

"The classics," Madison Blackberry's grandmother said approvingly, when she found Rockstar seated in the pale green velvet armchair with a tiny *Moby-Dick* on her lap.

Rockstar also read the miniature *LIFE* magazines from the 70s that were in the wooden magazine stand. Although they were out-of-date, they gave her a sense of the world beyond the dollhouse. She didn't like that world, but she wanted to understand it. Maybe this would help bring B.

Friend back to her.

After the disappearances, Miss Selene just wanted to change clothes. This made perfect sense to Miss Selene. The world was much too big. Especially for a doll! The idea of changing herself felt overwhelming.

And besides, in a way, changing clothes was changing herself. It might even change the world in a tiny way, mightn't it? Somehow make things just a tiny, tiny bit more magical?

Wildflower, Rockstar, and Miss Selene waited, trying to be as quiet and inconspicuous as possible, trying to come up with a plan so that Madison Blackberry would change

her mind and bring Guy and B. Friend
back.

Instead, one day, the dresses were
gone.

part three

ROSE

The dolls wandered
through their house
crying out,
"Where is the
lemon-yellow
satin chemise?"
"The bejeweled
green silk strapless
mermaid evening
gown with
the tulle tail?"

"Where is the blue feather poncho?" "The black velvet pearl-button-encrusted suit with the pink feather collar?"

For the first time they fully understood that Guy and B. Friend were gone and that nothing beautiful was left.⌉

Madison Blackberry had stored all the dresses away in a rose-covered hatbox. Although her mother bought her expensive clothes, she had nothing handmade by her grandmother, nothing even slightly magical. If she couldn't have a pink-and-silver chiffon cocoon jacket or lavender-and-gold silk kimono butterfly-wing sleeved dress, why should her dolls?

Of course, Miss Selene took it hardest of all. She knew clothes weren't the most important things in the world. But for many years she had used them to forget about other things. At the back of her mind, the main thing she had tried to forget rocked back and forth like the empty cradle in the nursery but she

peach velvet-and-chiffon bias-
ss with slits in the back for her
or herself.

ndmother held the sketches up
her crisp cotton blouse and
rocheted sweater with abalone
uttons, held them to her heart.
were confirmation of something
always wanted to believe: As a
rl, she had not really been alone,
ter the very worst thing had hap-
to her.

ndmother sat in front of the doll-
and talked. She said, "My name
; Wildflower knows that. She
ed to me when I was a girl. Came
he house. I was so excited! My

42

couldn't see exactly what it was, just as you couldn't see that the cradle was empty unless you leaned all the way over and peeked inside.

One day Wildflower noticed Miss Selene sitting naked by the cradle, rocking it gently back and forth with her foot and suddenly she knew what she could do to help. Perhaps she could not change the world, but she could do this one little thing to help Miss Selene!

When Grandmother came to visit, Wildflower wrote a note on a tiny scrap of paper with a tiny pencil from the roll-top desk and left it out for Grandmother to see.

Grandmother noticed the dead moss

in the garde
dusty shelve
curtains, a
lying on the

"'Dress,'
wondered w
us dresses?
Grandmoth
paper in tl
out for the

Early t
some sketc
see them,

Miss
dresses. ⁄
bridal gov
with a fi

an
cu
wi

aga
hai
she
Th
she
littl
ever
pen

(
hous
is R
belo
with

very own world where nothing could go wrong. Everything that was beautiful about the real world and none of the sadness. Even after my mother was killed during the war . . ."

The dolls heard the word *war* and shivered where they lay on the parquet floor.

"Even after that time, this house made me feel safe. But now look at you!" She picked up Wildflower, whose hair had come out of her braids and whose painted features were faded, and Rockstar, whose foot was turned backward on her leg.

Grandmother put them down and picked up Miss Selene.

43

"Where are your clothes?" Grandmother asked. "That little girl just doesn't understand, does she?"

And Wildflower wished and wished, as hard as she could, so hard that she thought she might break into pieces.

She did not wish for Guy or B. Friend to come back or for dresses or even for the thing Miss Selene had lost that she couldn't quite remember but that made her feel as empty as the empty cradle in the nursery.

Instead, Wildflower wished that Grandmother would make a dress for Madison Blackberry, and that she would love her the way Grandmother's mother had once loved Grandmother.

44

And that was what happened. Because even though someone is small, her wishes can be big and powerful, especially if the wishes are about love.

part four

LOVE

Grandmother
went and found
Madison Blackberry.
She showed her a
picture of her
mother, a faded
black-and-white
print of a lovely,
serious-seeming
woman with full
features and
pale eyes.

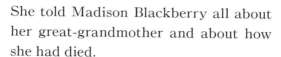

She told Madison Blackberry all about her great-grandmother and about how she had died.

"You look like her," Grandmother said.

Madison Blackberry looked at the photograph. Sometimes she felt as if her mother didn't care as much about her as she cared about her friends and her parties but at least Madison had a mother. She looked up and saw tears filling her grandmother's blue eyes with their light.

Madison Blackberry reached over and put her arms around

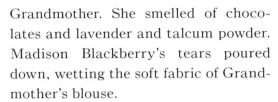

Grandmother. She smelled of chocolates and lavender and talcum powder.
Madison Blackberry's tears poured
down, wetting the soft fabric of Grandmother's blouse.

"Oh, little one, little one," Grandmother said.

It was the first time her grandmother had called her that. Little, like
the dolls in the dollhouse. Little, like
someone you want to protect and care
for and cannot help but love.

The next day Grandmother made
a dress for Madison Blackberry that
was even more beautiful than the new
clothes she made for Wildflower, Rockstar, and Miss Selene. The dolls were

not jealous; they saw Madison Blackberry's face and they were relieved.

Madison Blackberry went into the
storage closet. It was dark and dusty
and smelled sourly of mothballs. She
searched through the old shopping bags
and gift boxes and winter coats and, fi-
nally, Madison Blackberry found Guy.

Then she went searching for B.
Friend. Madison Blackberry never
found his arm or his ruined glasses but
she found the rest of him and she sewed
him back together to prevent more
stuffing from coming out of him.

And, last of all, Madison Blackberry
went into her underwear drawer and
took out the matchbox she had hidden

there. Do you know what was in that matchbox? The thing that Miss Selene missed but had forgotten because it was too painful to remember.

Madison Blackberry brought back all of the doll clothes from the rose-covered hatbox and put them into the wardrobe

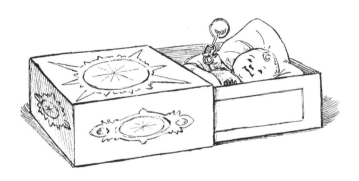

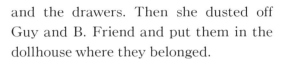

and the drawers. Then she dusted off
Guy and B. Friend and put them in the
dollhouse where they belonged.

Wildflower brushed her arm up
against Guy's arm. Her whole body tingled as if she were made of flesh and
not celluloid, or at least that was what
she imagined flesh tingled like. It did
not matter that he was a much newer
doll than she was, a younger soul with
darker skin and army fatigues.

"What was war like?" Wildflower
asked.

And Guy whispered, "War is being
blinded and locked in a box, unable to
see, hear, or touch you, my wildflower.
War is being reminded that you are

completely at the mercy of death at every moment, without the illusion that you are not. Without the distractions that make life worth living."

Rockstar dressed B. Friend's wounds with tiny cotton balls dipped in water and tiny cut-up Band-Aid strips that Madison Blackberry had given her. Then Rockstar read to him from the books she had discovered.

He said, "You have changed."

And she said, "I wanted to change. It's all I could do."

"I've changed, too," said B. Friend. "I can't touch the hollow of your back when we dance. I can't be of much help in the kitchen. If I lie next to you in

55

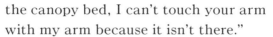
the canopy bed, I can't touch your arm with my arm because it isn't there."

"You can rest beside me, though," Rockstar said. And when Madison Blackberry put them into the canopy bed that night, side by side, staring up at the dark ceiling, that's exactly what they did.

As for Miss Selene: Madison Blackberry put Miss Selene's long-lost baby gently back into her arms, rather than in the cradle beside the wrought-iron bed, because Madison Blackberry

had always wished she could have slept like that with her mother, and Miss Selene and her baby lay together every night, wearing the matching lace nightgowns Grandmother had made for them.

That night, as if she knew, as if she had heard the secret voices of dolls, or the unspoken wish of her daughter, Madison Blackberry's mother came into Madison's room. She was not dressed for a party but wore blue jeans and a cotton T-shirt and there was no makeup on her face.

"I decided to stay home with you and Dallas George and your father tonight," she said. "Would you like me to read to you?"

Madison Blackberry nodded and then her mother sat on her bed with her arm around Madison and read to her from a little, worn, red-and-white book called *The Doll's House*, a book that had belonged to Madison's mother when she was a girl.

Madison's father was not away on a business trip that night. He had been home watching the news. He came into the room as Madison was falling asleep. He stood in the doorway, a tall shadow surrounded by light from the hall. Madison and her mother looked up at him. Then Madison's father spoke. His voice was soft with tears, almost unrecognizable.

"The war is over, my loves," he said.

Madison saw him through her half-closed eyes. She knew he was right; it was.

FRANCESCA LIA BLOCK,
winner of the prestigious Margaret A.
Edwards Award, is the author of
many acclaimed and bestselling
books, including WEETZIE BAT,
DANGEROUS ANGELS: *The Weetzie Bat
Books*, the collection of stories BLOOD
ROSES, the poetry collection HOW TO
(UN)CAGE A GIRL, and the novels THE
WATERS & THE WILD and PRETTY DEAD.
Her work is published around the
world. You can visit her online at
www.francescaliablock.com.

BARBARA McCLINTOCK has written and illustrated many acclaimed books for young readers, including ADÈLE & SIMON, DAHLIA, and MOLLY AND THE MAGIC WISHBONE. She is also the illustrator of many more, including Jim Aylesworth's retellings of THE TALE OF TRICKY FOX and THE GINGERBREAD MAN. She lives in Windham, Connecticut.

couldn't see exactly what it was, just as you couldn't see that the cradle was empty unless you leaned all the way over and peeked inside.

One day Wildflower noticed Miss Selene sitting naked by the cradle, rocking it gently back and forth with her foot and suddenly she knew what she could do to help. Perhaps she could not change the world, but she could do this one little thing to help Miss Selene!

When Grandmother came to visit, Wildflower wrote a note on a tiny scrap of paper with a tiny pencil from the roll-top desk and left it out for Grandmother to see.

Grandmother noticed the dead moss

in the garden, the dying bonsai tree, the dusty shelves, and the torn silk and lace curtains, and she saw the naked dolls lying on the floor of their house.

"'Dress,'" Grandmother read. She wondered what it meant: Dress us? Make us dresses? Dress up? Dress our wounds? Grandmother found some more scraps of paper in the rolltop desk and left them out for the dolls to tell her more.

Early the next morning there were some sketches, so faint you could hardly see them, on the scraps of paper.

Miss Selene had drawn three dresses. A white lace Victorian-style bridal gown for Wildflower, a red suit with a faux-fur collar for Rockstar,

41

and a peach velvet-and-chiffon bias-cut dress with slits in the back for her wings for herself.

Grandmother held the sketches up against her crisp cotton blouse and hand-crocheted sweater with abalone shell buttons, held them to her heart. They were confirmation of something she had always wanted to believe: As a little girl, she had not really been alone, even after the very worst thing had happened to her.

Grandmother sat in front of the doll-house and talked. She said, "My name is Rose; Wildflower knows that. She belonged to me when I was a girl. Came with the house. I was so excited! My